SPLAT!

Jon Burgerman

Everything splatted by

ross

Dial Books for Young Readers

What happens when you turn the page?

Good work!

What will happen this time?

That's right, congratulations!

That wasn't very funny, was it?

I'm getting hungry.

are you?

Who else likes sandwiches?

We love insect sandwiches.

No more splats,
right?

We got everyone ice cream!

Author's note:
No little birds, bugs, or green fluffy characters
were hurt in the making of this book.
A few pies were destroyed, though.

SPLAT! is dedicated to You Jung

Dial Books for Young Readers
Penguin Young Readers Group
An imprint of Penguin Random House LLC
375 Hudson Street
New York, New York 10014

ISBN 9780735228764

Manufactured in China.

Export edition ISBN: 9780192749543
eBook ISBN: 9780192749550

1 3 5 7 9 10 8 6 4 2

Designed by Jon Burgerman and Holly Fulbrook
Main text set in Burgerman 1.7 with the permission of the author